Seek and Find
Princess

McKinley,
Congrats on the birth of
your baby sister! Welcome
Ainsley!

Love
Nan & Papa
XO

BARRON'S

Princess Sabrina and the Royal Ball

Princess Sabrina's older sister Princess Emilia is planning a magnificent ball, and all of her friends will be there in their most beautiful dresses. But there are no new dresses left for Sabrina! How can she go to the ball without a special dress?

Luckily, you're here to help Princess Sabrina gather the items she will need to make a brand-new dress. There are special things to find on every page.

Remember, the Princess never goes anywhere without her Royal Charm Bracelet. Collect the five different charms each time she travels to another part of the Kingdom. The charms are:

- a heart
- a star
- a lock
- a leaf
- a strawberry

Also, look for the five purple flowers from her bracelet in every picture.

As you search for the things that Princess Sabrina needs, keep an eye out for a forgetful courtier. He has lost some of the Queen's most treasured possessions.

On the last page of this book, there is a list of things that the courtier has misplaced.

Can you find them all?

Super Seek and Find

All the items on this page can be found somewhere in this book. Look through the pages to find them.

Some of the items might pop up in unusual places! Help the courtier find the hidden items so he can return them to the Queen.

6 Blue pigs 4 Pandas 9 Hedgehogs 5 Cheeses

8 Bats 2 Swans 11 Pencils 1 Bucket

3 Shells 5 Gray moustaches 13 Polka dot hankies 4 Pairs of glasses

6 Cupcakes 3 Horseshoes 1 Snake 2 Pink rabbits

First edition for North America published in 2014 by Barron's Educational Series, Inc.

Text, design, and illustrations copyright © Hinkler Books 2013

First published in 2013 by Hinkler Books.

All inquiries should be addressed to:
Barron's Educational Series, Inc.
250 Wireless Boulevard
Hauppauge, New York 11788
www.barronseduc.com

Authors: Rachel Elliot and Lisa Regan
Illustrator: Helen Prole
ISBN: 978-0-7641-6697-6
Library of Congress Control No.: 2013943867
Date of Manufacture: December 2013
Manufactured by: Hung Hing Printing, Shenzhen, China

Printed in China

9 8 7 6 5 4 3 2 1

This product conforms to ASTM F-963 and all applicable CPSC and CPSIA 2008 standards. No lead or phthalate hazard.

By royal invitation

Princess Emilia is hosting a ball.

"Royal invitations go out to you all!"

Sabrina's excited, although there's a problem:

"My dresses don't fit, I need a new one!"

Help find her charms, then head for the city.

Find a new dress that makes her look pretty.

Watch the Queen's courtier taking the blame.

He's lost many things and must find them again.

Can you help Sabrina find these items?

 **6** Invitations

 **4** Picture frames

 **13** Doves

 **5** Swords

 **7** Jester hats

 **1** Clock

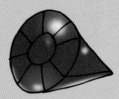 **3** Emeralds

 **12** Balls

 **8** Cats

 **11** Pears

Horse and carriage

Sabrina is going to look for a gown.

The carriage awaits for the trip into town.

Four prancing horses so fine, white, and strong

Trot on ahead and pull her along.

The courtier needs to hurry up, too.

He has a most urgent job he must do.

Can you help
Sabrina find
these items?

 **1** Coach

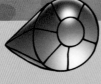 **8** Sapphires

 **13** Yellow roses

 16 Bees

3 Cloaks **8** Helmets **6** Straw hats **4** Horses **12** Mice

Some bad news

Princess Sabrina arrives at the store,

Hoping to choose from dresses galore.

But it's a disaster! The hangers are bare.

She looks around and sees no dresses there!

"I'll make you a gown, just bring me the things—

Flowers or feathers or shiny sequins."

Can you help Sabrina find these items?

2 Sapphire earrings

10 Bangles

8 Shopping bags

6 Bathing suits

4 Long gloves

7 Purses

2 Lamps

8 Tiaras

12 Knitting needles

11 Stripey shoes

The beauty salon

Sit in the salon, a wonderful place,

They can polish nails and make up your face.

The courtier smiles from his hiding spot.

He sees the hairdo the Princess has got.

She's found a pretty headband to go in her hair,

To start off an outfit with style and flair.

Can you help Sabrina find these items?

 **6** Combs

 18 Cotton balls

 **3** Cups and saucers

 **2** Hairbrushes

 **4** Fancy headbands

 **6** Hair ribbons

 **10** Butterfly clips

 **3** Nail files

 **11** Nail polishes

 7 Crowns

Can you help Sabrina find these items?

6 Handbags **9** Ducks **16** Marbles **2** Watches

Shoe shopping!

The Princess needs shoes for her dainty feet,

The ones she tries on are ever so sweet.

Feathers from peacocks cover the toes,

Her feet will look gorgeous wherever she goes!

The shoe seller says she should try to find more.

These feathers were found at the lake, on the shore.

5 Cinnamon buns

12 Shoeboxes

8 Boots

6 Rubies

7 Pearls

Finding feathers

Princess Sabrina is delighted to see

Peacocks aplenty roaming happy and free.

Some of their feathers have dropped to the ground.

She picks what she needs, they're all around.

Over the bridge she hears music and laughter.

It comes from the fair—they'll have what she's after.

Can you help Sabrina find these items?

 **6** Clouds

 **9** Sheep

 **1** Bridge

 **3** Fish

 **11** Feathers

 **2** Butterflies

 **4** Boats

 **12** Apples

 **16** Robins

 **6** Peacocks

Winning a prize

The courtier has fun doing loop after loop,

While the Princess is busy throwing a hoop.

She steadies her hand and narrows her eyes.

The hoop lands on the target—she wins a prize!

This jar of sequins will help with her gown.

It will shimmer and shine, the talk of the town.

Can you help Sabrina find these items?

2 Birds

17 Candy apples

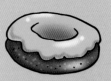
7 Doughnuts

5 Ladybug cars

3 Hot dogs

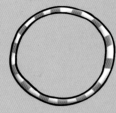
10 Hoops

9 Flags

4 Red flowers

12 Balloons

1 Giant slide

Picnic in the park

Leaving the fair, Sabrina needs lunch.

She meets her friends who have goodies to munch.

Towers of chocolates, apples, and cake.

The courtier hands out cherries to take.

They play hide and seek, they're having such fun.

But the dress still needs work, Sabrina must run.

Can you help Sabrina find these items?

 1 Butterfly

 3 Pitchers

 **9** Roses

 **18** Cupcakes

 **5** Carrot cakes

 2 Pockets

 **7** Drink umbrellas

 **6** Beetles

 **8** Rabbits

 **11** Peeping princesses

Can you help Sabrina find these items?

1 Wheelbarrow **3** Shears **4** Watering cans **19** Tall flowers

The palace gardens

Back at the palace, no time to stop.

Sabrina must send all her things to the shop.

The gardener finds flowers sure to impress.

To join the fine feathers on her new dress.

The courtier is still working hard for the Queen,

But some of her lost things have not yet been seen.

11 Shovels   **10** Pigeons   **4** Oranges   **16** Plant pots   **2** Lizards

Band practice

The whole palace staff are involved in the ball.
Sabrina hears music as she walks through the hall.
It's the Royal Band, who are very excited.
They have practiced non-stop since they were invited.
The leader smiles as she gives a bow.
"I hope you're in tune, enjoy watching our show."

Can you help Sabrina find these items?

4 Stools

6 Crowns

3 Music books

14 Carrots

15 Bows

5 Jars

11 Blackbirds

9 Pineapples

1 Harp

2 Trumpets

Sabrina's bedchamber

With ten minutes to spare, she lies down for a rest.

Then all of her friends come by to get dressed.

They laugh and they chatter, and check on their hair.

"Will Prince Charming be here? What will he wear?"

Here's Sabrina's new dress. "Let's see if it fits.

It's gorgeous! Just perfect! I love it to bits!"

Can you help Sabrina find these items?

2 Shawls

1 Diamond ring

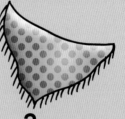

2 Hand mirrors

4 Pearl earrings

11 Lipsticks

9 Guinea pigs

6 Potatoes

7 Blushes

17 Rhinestones

11 Frilly scarves

The royal ball!

Emilia is delighted to dance with the Prince.

She playfully grins at her sister and winks.

The King and the Queen are there having fun,

The courtier is resting—his search is now done.

Sabrina is happy. It has all come together—

Her bracelet, her outift, and every last feather!

Can you help Sabrina find these items?

 **10** Glasses

 **3** Bow ties

 **5** Cameras

 **6** Candles

 11 Moons

 **4** Peaked hats

 **8** Silver stars

 **14** Coins

 **7** Curly straws

 **2** Pink ball gowns

Super Seek and Find

All the items on this page can be found somewhere in this book. Look through the pages to find them.

Some of the items might pop up in unusual places! Help the courtier find the hidden items so he can return them to the Queen.

6 Blue pigs

4 Pandas

9 Hedgehogs

5 Cheeses

8 Bats

2 Swans

11 Pencils

1 Bucket

3 Shells

5 Gray moustaches

13 Polka dot hankies

4 Pairs of glasses

6 Cupcakes

3 Horseshoes

1 Snake

2 Pink rabbits